SHE'S MY SISTER

SHE'S MY SISTER

JANE CLAYPOOL MINER

2.3-4.5   3.90

Fearon Education, a division of
David S. Lake Publishers
Belmont, California 94002

CRISIS SERIES

A DAY AT A TIME
MIRACLE OF TIME
MOUNTAIN FEAR
NEW BEGINNING
SHE'S MY SISTER
SPLIT DECISION

Fearon Education Edition

Senior development editor: Janet Joers
Managing editor: Maura Okamoto
Content editor: Dr. Howard Schroeder
Production editor: Robert E. Wanetick
Manufacturing manager: Susan M. Fox
Cover and text designer: Baker Street Productions
Illustrator: Vista III Design

ISBN–0–8224–1655–7
Printed in the United States of America

1.9 8 7 6 5 4

CONTENTS

CHAPTER 1

Mary Lou looked helplessly at her parents. Tears ran down her face as she tried to explain how she felt. "You just don't know what kids are like. Once they find out I have a retarded sister, no one will want me for a friend. They'll talk about me behind my back. They'll laugh at Judy."

Her mother shook her head. "You're not listening. Judy will be in a different part of the school. She won't be anywhere near your classes."

"You're the one who doesn't understand," Mary Lou answered. "They'll find out. They always do. Besides, Judy always . . . she hangs on me, Mother. I hate that."

"This is getting us nowhere," her father said. "The fact is that Judy comes home next week." He rose from his chair and went toward the hallway. "I'm going to mow the lawn. Let's get something done around here. The day's almost over."

Mary Lou frowned at her father. That was

always the way he ended arguments. He just got up and walked away. It was no good trying to talk to her mother. She would never understand either.

Mary Lou decided to get out of the kitchen before her mother asked her to do the breakfast dishes or something. "I guess I'll go to the lake," she said.

"I'd like some help," her mother said.

Mary Lou answered crossly, "Mother, there are only two more weeks before school starts. Don't ruin the last part of my vacation."

"You act as though it is all our fault that Judy is coming home," her mother said. "Don't you understand that the school officials are the ones who decided that Judy is ready for regular home life?"

"Judy doesn't have to come here. She could go to a halfway house in another town," Mary Lou said. "You are the one who decided she could come here."

Her mother turned white and said quickly, "I know you're upset, but you don't really mean that. You wouldn't want your sister to live with strangers."

Mary Lou saw from the white face and thin lips that her mother was very angry. She always tried

to sound understanding when the subject of Judy came up. But her mother wasn't really understanding at all. It seemed to Mary Lou that her mother had always loved Judy more. Her mother had nearly died when they'd put Judy in the special school ten years ago.

After finishing the dishes, Mary Lou left the kitchen and went to her bedroom to dress for the lake. As she pulled her jeans on over her swimsuit, she thought about her problem. How could she ever go to the same school as her sister, Judy?

Judy was two years older than Mary Lou, but

she was smaller and looked younger. Though Judy looked more normal than many of the other children in the school where she lived, she did look different. She was short and her face was very round. Her eyes were different, too. But the main thing was that Judy would never be very smart. She was eighteen and had the mind of a six-year-old.

Mary Lou tried to love her sister. When she went to visit Judy at the special school, she was always nice to her. She let Judy comb her long, blonde hair and hug her as much as she wanted to. She took Judy on walks and talked to her about the things they saw. But she didn't like to take Judy to the village or out to eat. People stared and Mary Lou hated that.

As she thought about her problem, Mary Lou looked in the mirror. She brushed her hair and tied it back with a piece of pink ribbon. Then suddenly she stopped moving and looked closely in the mirror. Her eyes clouded for just a second. She was so lucky that she wasn't like Judy!

CHAPTER 2

It was one of those beautiful August days when the sun was hot but a cool lake breeze kept everyone feeling good. Mary Lou walked up and down the water's edge until she saw a group of her friends. She dropped her towel beside Sally, Mark, and Chris. Over on a blanket, Sue and Ellen were playing cards.

The kids were talking about school as she sat down. "Let's talk about something else," Mary

Lou said. "School is two whole weeks away."

"But Sally is going to leave Hill City and transfer to West High," Chris said. "What do you think of that?"

"They have a better science department," Sally explained. "Now that we have an open transfer program, I might as well go to the school that will help me the most. I'll live with my grandmother and come home weekends."

Before Mary Lou could say anything, Sue and Ellen began laughing at each other over the card

game. Sue tossed her cards at Ellen and said, "You're such a retard! I'm not going to play with you anymore."

Sue jumped up and said to everyone, "Did you hear that we're going to get a whole lot of retards at Hill City next year? Ellen's going to transfer into that class."

Sue started running toward the water. Ellen jumped up and called, "You think I'm dumb? Well, see what I figure out to do to you!"

She chased Sue into the water and tried to push

her under. The two girls yelled, screamed, and splashed each other. Sally, Mark, and Chris watched from where they were sitting.

Mary Lou's face was frozen into a smile. This was what her folks would never understand. She was sitting with some of the most popular kids at school and their favorite put-down was to call each other "retards." They would never even dream that one of their crowd could actually have a retarded sister.

Mary Lou sat on her towel and hugged her knees. Even though the sun was very hot, she shivered. What if Sue or Ellen found out that Judy was her sister?

"I guess they are going to have a special school for retarded kids this year," Sally said. She was talking to Mary Lou, who didn't answer.

"They'll use the old wing," Chris replied. His father was a teacher, so he knew all about the school. "My dad says they'll stick pretty much to themselves."

"Sometimes retarded kids go to regular classes," Sally said.

"Yeah, but they're just sort of slow," Chris added. "These kids are really slow. And weird looking — you know."

Mary Lou stared out at the blue water and

wished she could swim off to another part of the world. She would like to live on a desert island, all alone. She would rather live on coconuts and bananas and never go to school at all. She would rather be lonely than feel this uncomfortable.

"Want to go for a swim?" Sally asked.

Mary Lou shook her head no. She didn't feel

like swimming or talking or anything else. The
awful secret of her sister was making her throat
go closed.

"You look very sad," Sally said. "Thinking
about starting school again?"

"I am thinking about school," Mary Lou replied. "I'm thinking about changing to West too."

"Great!" Sally said. "It would be so wonderful to start out with a friend. I hate the thought of meeting all new people."

Better to make new friends than to lose old ones, Mary Lou thought. She had been afraid that having her sister Judy at her school would cost her all her friends. Today proved it.

CHAPTER 3

Mary Lou's father said it was the worst idea he'd ever heard, but her mother backed her up. After a two day argument, her folks agreed that Mary Lou could transfer to West High. It was then that Mary Lou told them she wanted to live with her Aunt Helen.

That caused another two days of arguments. Her father thought she should live at home and spend two hours a day on the bus. "You could read," he told her.

Mary Lou didn't want that. She told her folks it was because she'd never be able to be in school activities. The truth was, she didn't want to have

to bring her friends home. There they would see Judy.

Finally, a week before school started, her folks agreed that they would talk to Helen about it. Mary Lou smiled. She knew Helen would say yes. Helen and she were good friends.

On Saturday morning, they all went over to Helen's apartment. Helen listened quietly as Mary Lou's mother explained the problem. Mary Lou looked around the large, colorful room where she would be living. She was sure she would like living with Helen.

Helen lived a lot like the way Mary Lou wanted to live when she grew up. She had interesting paintings on the walls and lots of pretty clothes. Though she had many dates, Helen didn't seem very interested in getting married. She liked her job and had several friends. Helen was fun to be with and seemed a lot younger than her mother. In truth, there was only three years difference between them. But when Mary Lou was with Helen, she always felt as though she was with a friend.

Helen said yes as quickly as Mary Lou expected

she would. But she didn't seem very happy about it. "You'll have to do your share of the work," her aunt warned. "And since you'll be sleeping on the couch, it will be very important for you to do your work on time."

Mary Lou felt her face go red. It was true that she didn't always help with the housework as quickly as her mother wanted. But she would be different at Helen's. Living with Helen would be almost like living in her own apartment with a roommate. "I'll help out," she promised.

Helen suggested that Mary Lou move some of her clothes and things in tomorrow. "Your folks will have their hands full with Judy," she said. "You can spend next week here with me."

Everyone agreed that was a good idea. Mary Lou was especially glad to be out of the house before Judy arrived. She knew that Judy would be very sad if Mary Lou packed up and left after she got there.

Each Saturday morning for the last ten years, her mother and father had made the long drive to the special school to see Judy. At first, Mary Lou and her brother Tim went with them. Tim was in the army now, and Mary Lou often had other things to do. She hadn't seen Judy for three months. None of her friends knew she had a

retarded sister because they'd moved to this town after Judy went away. If her plan worked, they would never know.

Only her mother seemed to think the plan was a bad idea. "But Judy will want to see Mary Lou when she comes home," she said. "She'll be so disappointed."

"Mary Lou has a right to her own life," her father said.

Mary Lou smiled. Usually it was her mother who took her side. It was good to have her father on her side for once. She felt that her parents tried hard to be fair, but she was sure they loved Judy more. Maybe it was normal to love a handicapped child more. She wasn't sure about that. All she knew was that she was going to West High, where there was no chance that Judy could spoil things for her.

The next morning, Mary Lou's folks drove her and several suitcases full of clothes to Helen's house. Her mother kissed her good-bye and said, "I'd like to help you settle in, but we have to hurry. Judy will be expecting us."

"That's OK," Mary Lou said. She meant it. She really wanted to be alone in Helen's apartment. Her aunt was at work and wouldn't be back until five. That gave Mary Lou all day alone. It would be great fun.

Mary Lou promised her mother she would call every day. She stood in the doorway and watched as her parents walked to their car. When they turned the corner, Mary Lou went inside.

She had been in Helen's apartment many times, but this was different. She felt grown-up and wonderful as she walked around the room, looking at the paintings and books. She spent the rest of the morning looking through Helen's records and playing the ones that interested her. At noon, she made herself lunch and called her friend Sally on the telephone.

After Mary Lou listened to a very long story

about the troubles Sally was having with her boy-friend, Sally asked her a question. "I've told you the real reason I'm going to West is so I can break up with my boyfriend," she said. "Now it's your turn. What's the real reason you're going? I know you're not that interested in the special science program."

For a minute, Mary Lou thought about telling Sally the truth. She liked Sally a lot, but she didn't know if she should trust her. She decided to tell a lie. "I guess I'm not getting along with my folks that well. My aunt will be a lot more fun to live with."

When she finished talking to Sally, she decided to surprise Helen and start supper. She went to the kitchen cabinets and looked for something that she could cook. There was nothing in the refrigerator but eggs and cheese. Helen didn't seem to have much food. Finally, she found some spaghetti and some canned clams. That would be the start of an Italian dish. Maybe, if she had time, she would go to the store and get something special for dessert.

Mary Lou was in the kitchen when Helen came home. She didn't hear the door open, so she was surprised when Helen came up behind her.

"Your clothes are all over the living room," Helen said.

Mary Lou jumped in surprise and dropped a can of tomato sauce on the floor. Helen didn't look very happy as Mary Lou stammered, "I'm sorry. I'll wipe it up."

"I tried to call you all afternoon," Helen said. "The phone was always busy."

"I was talking to a friend," Mary Lou explained. "I didn't expect you to call."

"I don't want you to tie up the telephone like that. I called to invite you to join me and a friend for supper," her aunt said. "But it seems like you've got other plans."

"Oh, no," Mary Lou said. "I'd love to come with you."

But Helen looked very firm as she said, "No. I imagine you will want to clean the kitchen and you still need to put your clothes away."

"I'll do it later," Mary Lou begged. "It will only take me a minute to get ready."

"Things are a mess," Helen said.

"Please, Helen, don't be a grouch. I'll get it done tomorrow, I promise."

Her aunt finally agreed but she didn't look happy. Mary Lou promised herself that she'd have to be more careful in the future.

CHAPTER 4

Living with her aunt wasn't as great as Mary Lou had hoped. In the first place, Helen was more cross than she'd expected. It seemed to Mary Lou that she snapped at her all the time. One other thing that bothered Mary Lou was that Helen was bossier than her mother.

Her mother never told her where to hang her coat or how to wash dishes. Helen couldn't watch Mary Lou do anything without telling her a better way to do it. They had their first big fight about how to cut butter.

It was the third day that Mary Lou had been there. At dinner that night, the conversation had been mostly about what Mary Lou did during the day.

"Did you get the laundry done?" Helen asked.

"Yes."

"Did you get your clothes ready for school?"

"Yes." That was a lie, but Mary Lou wanted to

avoid trouble. She added, "I still need some sweaters from home. Will you pick them up on your way home from work tomorrow?"

"Sorry, no. I'm busy tomorrow afternoon. You can bring them with you this weekend, after you visit your family," Helen suggested.

"I'm not sure I'm going home this weekend," Mary Lou said.

"Well, I'm sure," replied Helen. She sliced some butter from the cube for her toast. "I can use a little peace and quiet."

It made Mary Lou feel bad when Helen said she'd rather be alone. She decided to ignore that thought, and sliced some butter for her toast.

"Why do you cut from that end?" Helen asked. "I'd already started on the other end."

Mary Lou stared at the square of butter in front of her. She wanted to ask why Helen even bothered to notice such a small thing. "It doesn't matter," she said. "No one will see that the butter is crooked."

"I see it," Helen said. "You should always cut the butter from the same end."

"Wow! Are you bossy!" yelled Mary Lou. She tried to laugh but she was really very angry. "Do you tell people who work for you what to do all the time?"

"The point is," her aunt continued, "why not slice the butter from the same end? It looks neater and it's just as easy. Sometimes, you don't think, Mary Lou. You've got to learn to be more alert."

"Like you," Mary Lou said. She was really angry now. "You're always so alert. So right! You're always right." She jumped up from the table and went into the living room to watch television.

She half expected that her aunt would come in later and try to make up, but she didn't. Instead, her aunt washed the dishes and went out.

Mary Lou was very unhappy. There was nothing good on television and she didn't have anyone to talk to. She tried to read, but the books weren't very interesting. She thought of calling one of her friends on the telephone, but she was afraid Helen might try to call her and get angry.

Mary Lou cried a little that night. She wanted to call her mother and talk to her, but she decided not to. Her mother would want her to move home. Besides that, both times she'd called home, she'd had to talk to Judy. Each time, Judy asked when she was coming home. Finally, Mary Lou took a bath and fixed her nails.

The next morning, Helen was angry because she'd used her nail polish. "I'll buy you some

more!" Mary Lou shouted.

"Don't shout at me," Helen said. "I'm not your mother. I don't have to put up with it."

"I don't shout at my mother," Mary Lou said.

"No, because she does whatever you want," Helen answered quickly. She slammed the door as she went to work.

That evening, Helen said, "I want to talk to you seriously, Mary Lou."

Mary Lou was still angry, but she listened quietly as her aunt talked. "My job is very important to me. I work very hard and I love it. But at night, I like to have peace and quiet in my home. I

can't spend my time fighting with you."

"I didn't start it," said Mary Lou.

"It doesn't matter who started it," Helen answered. "The point is, I don't want to fight. Today, at work, I shouted at one of the best persons in the business. I can't do that again. My work is too important to me."

Mary Lou wanted to ask if she wasn't important, too. She decided Helen would just tell her again that she wasn't her mother. "I'll try to do things your way," Mary Lou said.

Helen nodded and stood up. "Good. Now, for a start, let me help you put away the sweaters I

picked up from your folks' house."

"Oh thanks," Mary Lou said. She saw that her aunt was trying to make up. After all, she'd done what Mary Lou asked her to do.

"Your mother misses you," Helen said. "And she said that Judy asks about you all the time. They'll be glad to see you tomorrow."

"I thought I'd go home on Saturday morning," Mary Lou said.

Helen shook her head. "No. Friday afternoon will be better. I have company coming for dinner and I'd like to be alone with my friend. You understand."

As she talked, Helen opened the chest that sat beside the pull-out couch. It was where Mary Lou kept her folded clothes. Helen looked down at the drawer and said, "This is horrible. You'll have to straighten it out."

"The drawer is empty below," said Mary Lou. "I'll put the sweaters in there."

"But this has to be straightened out right away," Helen said. "It's impossible."

"Helen, no one will see it," Mary Lou said.

"That's just like you," Helen answered. "As long as no one can see it, as long as you can get away with it, as long as you don't get caught."

"That's not fair!" Mary Lou cried.

"You're shouting again," Helen said. "I just can't have this. I have to have peace and quiet."

"All you think about is yourself," Mary Lou answered. "You never think about me."

"That's just the point," Helen answered. "I do think about you but I think about myself, too. Your mother never thinks about anyone but her children. I'm afraid you're really very spoiled,

Mary Lou. And you only care how things look,
not how they really are."

Mary Lou looked at her aunt with tears in her
eyes. If she had been in her own home, she
would have run to her room and cried. Here, she
didn't have a room of her own. "I think I'll take a
walk," she said.

"Not until you straighten out this drawer and

put your sweaters away," Helen said.

But Mary Lou was out the door before her aunt could finish her sentence. She wasn't listening. She was tired of listening to her aunt. She wanted to be alone to think. Mary Lou wanted to take a good long walk and see if she couldn't figure out what to do. The way things were going, she had to do something.

CHAPTER 5

Her aunt didn't seem very surprised when Mary Lou told her she was moving home. Helen said, "I guess I'm hard to live with, Mary Lou. I'm sorry about that."

"It will be better to go back to Hill City," Mary Lou continued. "All my old friends are there."

"I'll help you pack," her aunt said. When they were finished, they drove to Mary Lou's house.

Mary Lou was very glad her father didn't say, "I told you so," when he saw her. Instead, he held her very tightly and said, "I missed you, kiddo. Glad you're home."

"Put your things in your room," her mother said after she kissed her.

Mary Lou picked up her suitcase and went quickly to her bedroom to put her clothes back into the closets and drawers. It wasn't any time until Judy came in to help her. Mary Lou was surprised at how glad she was to see Judy. It didn't even bother her when Judy hugged her and asked, "Can I help?"

Mary Lou showed Judy how to help her put her

clothes away. Judy made a few mistakes but most of the things she did were right. "They taught you a lot at that school," Mary Lou said to her sister.

Judy nodded happily. As Mary Lou stood looking down at her retarded sister, she wondered what life must be like for Judy. Was it awful? She didn't think so. Judy usually seemed happy and cheerful.

"Come on, I'll fix your hair," Mary Lou said.

For the next few minutes, Mary Lou combed

Judy's hair. It was short and brown, not long and blonde like Mary Lou's. Even so, Mary Lou put a pink ribbon in Judy's hair. Judy liked to have the same things as Mary Lou had.

The two girls were looking at a book when Helen came to say good-bye. Helen kissed Judy, then Mary Lou, on the cheek. "I learned a lot about myself last week, Mary Lou," she said. "I hope you did, too." Then she laughed and said, "I know one thing. I'm not going to get married soon. It's easier to live alone."

After Helen left, their mother called Judy to help her in the kitchen. Mary Lou knew that her mother would keep Judy away from her for the rest of the day. Ever since the beginning, her folks had tried very hard to let Mary Lou lead a normal life.

Mary Lou flopped on the bed and stared at the ceiling. Before Judy went off to the special school, life hadn't been normal at all. Judy had been a lot of trouble to everyone. Mary Lou hoped that things would be easier now. She knew the school was proud of the work they'd done and what they'd taught Judy.

About four o'clock, the phone rang and it was for Mary Lou. It was her friend John. He wanted to know what she thought about a going-away party for Sally and her. He thought it could be at

his house tomorrow night.

"It would be just for Sally," Mary Lou said. "I'm staying at Hill City High."

John seemed glad at hearing the news. They were having a nice talk when Judy came up to the phone. "Is that Helen?" she said. "I want to talk." Before Mary Lou could do anything, Judy

grabbed the telephone and said, "I'll talk."

Mary Lou pushed the button down to cut off the conversation. Then she grabbed the telephone away from Judy and shouted, "No! No!! Get away!"

Judy began to cry and her mother rushed from the kitchen. She put her arm around Judy and said, "I'm sorry, honey. Come with me."

"I can't even have a regular telephone conversation," Mary Lou yelled.

"I'm sorry, honey," her mother said. Her face was white and tired. Her eyes looked very big.

Suddenly, Mary Lou felt ashamed of herself. She remembered that Helen had said she yelled at her mother. Mary Lou had to admit that it was true. "It's all right, Mom," she said. "Don't worry. It's just that I kind of like this boy and I guess I got nervous. I should be the one to apologize."

Her mother took Judy to the kitchen and Mary Lou called John back on the telephone. They arranged for the party to be the next night. John asked, "Would you rather have it at your house? You've got that big room in the basement."

"Oh, no," Mary Lou said. "Your house is better."

She put the telephone down and went back to her room. She would never be able to have another party at her house. She would never be able to invite anyone home after school. No one could ever know about Judy.

CHAPTER 6

Living with Judy was much easier than Mary Lou remembered. Her mother also seemed happier now that Judy was home. She sang around the house and laughed more often. One day, about a month after school had begun, Mary Lou talked to her mother about it.

"It's not just because Judy is home, you know," said her mother, smiling. "I don't know what Helen did to you, but you're much easier to live with. You hang up your clothes. You do your jobs faster. I'll never be able to thank you enough."

Mary Lou laughed. It was true that since she'd lived with Helen, she had learned to be more helpful. She was also glad to be home.

"It's all working out so well," her mother said happily. "Judy really does know how to take better care of herself than she used to. She isn't as much trouble. And, of course, she's in school all day." She hugged Mary Lou and said, "Oh, it's all working out all right, isn't it? I told you it would."

Mary Lou nodded. So far, her mother had been right about the most important thing. She never saw Judy at school. And none of her friends knew she had a retarded sister. If only that stayed the same, Mary Lou told herself, she would not complain.

Having Judy home was ruining her social life, though. Ever since she'd started back to school, she'd been making excuses not to see people. She knew she wasn't as friendly as she used to be. She also knew she was losing friends.

And then, a week later, one of the special kids got lost and walked into the school cafeteria during lunch. Several students pointed and some of them laughed. Mary Lou's heart pounded when she thought about what might have happened if the special kid had been Judy. Right then she decided not to eat lunch in the cafeteria anymore. She started skipping lunches and staying in the library, where she could read.

Even though she didn't go to the cafeteria, she knew it might happen in some other way. There was a fire drill one day. Mary Lou's class was very close to the kids in the special class. Mary Lou could see Judy standing next to her teacher. Quickly, Mary Lou turned and moved behind a very tall boy. Judy wasn't looking for her and she didn't see her.

Mary Lou began to worry all the time. She would awaken in the middle of the night and know that she'd just had a bad dream about her sister. My sister, my problem, she said to herself.

Mary Lou's worst fear was that Judy would see

her in school and run up to hug her. She could almost hear Judy saying, "My sister, my sister." She could almost feel Judy giving her a big, happy hug.

Mary Lou worried so much that it was almost as bad as if it had happened. The worst thing about it was that there was no one in the world that she could talk to about her fears. Though she and her Aunt Helen were friends again, Mary Lou knew her aunt would not understand. She knew it was stupid to go over the whole thing with her folks again. And she certainly couldn't talk to any of her friends about it.

Finally, just before Christmas vacation, her worst fears happened. Mary Lou's teacher asked her to get some books from the basement. On her way downstairs she had to go through a long, empty hallway near the special class. At the other end of the hallway, Mary Lou saw Judy with a blue pass. Judy didn't see her though, so Mary Lou quickly turned to go the other way. As she turned, two boys walked up to Judy. One of them asked the other, "This your girlfriend, Tim?"

Mary Lou turned the corner and stopped. She peeped around the wall and watched what was going to happen next. The boy named Tim said, "Sure she is." He put his arm around Judy and said, "Come on, Sweetie. Give me a kiss."

Both boys laughed very loudly. Judy looked from one boy to the other. She seemed to understand that the boys were laughing at her. She looked as though she might cry.

Mary Lou watched sadly. She hoped that Judy would turn around and go back to the room she came from. She hoped that the boys would get tired of their joke and go away. She didn't know either boy very well, but she did know that Ellen dated Tim. If he found out Judy was her sister, the whole school would quickly know it.

"Get out of here," she told herself. But she could not move.

Each boy took one of Judy's arms. Tim said, "Oh, sweetie, don't go with that one. He's no good. Stay with me."

The other boy pretended to be heartbroken and said, "No, no, sweetheart. Stay with me. Be my valentine."

Mary Lou knew they weren't really bad guys. They wouldn't hurt Judy, she told herself. She decided she could just leave.

Mary Lou started to walk away. She went three steps and then stopped. It was no good. Suddenly it didn't matter if everyone in the school knew about Judy. She couldn't go off and leave her sister like that. Judy might be in trouble!

Mary Lou turned around. She stepped out into the hall and pretended to see Judy for the first time. She called to her sister, "Hi, Judy. What are you doing?"

Tim looked surprised. "Hi, Mary Lou. Do you know her?" He asked.

"Judy is my sister," Mary Lou said in a clear voice.

"But she's . . ." the other boy started.

"She's my sister," Mary Lou repeated, bending down so Judy could hug her.